this book belongs to:

For all unicornologists, past and present
– Dr Temisa Seraphini

Thank you to Lilly, Harriet, Joanna and everyone
at Nobrow for giving me the opportunity to illustrate such
a wonderful book, and for teaching me so much.

And thank you to Leon Rozelaar, my mum, dad and my family and
friends for their tireless support, enthusiasm and belief in me.
– Sophie Robin

This is a first edition published in 2021 by Flying Eye Books, an imprint
of Nobrow Ltd. 27 Westgate Street, London, E8 3RL.

Text © Sangma Francis 2019
Illustrations © Sophie Robin 2019

Temisa Seraphini is the pen name of Sangma Francis. Sangma Francis and
Sophie Robin have asserted their rights under the Copyright, Designs and Patents Act,
1988, to be identified as the Author and Illustrator of this Work.

1 3 5 7 9 10 8 6 4 2

Published in the US by Nobrow (US) Inc.
Printed in Poland on FSC® certified paper.

ISBN: 978-1-83874-050-4
www.flyingeyebooks.com

The Secret Lives of
UNICORNS

Dr Temisa Seraphini and Sophie Robin

FLYING EYE BOOKS
London I Los Angeles

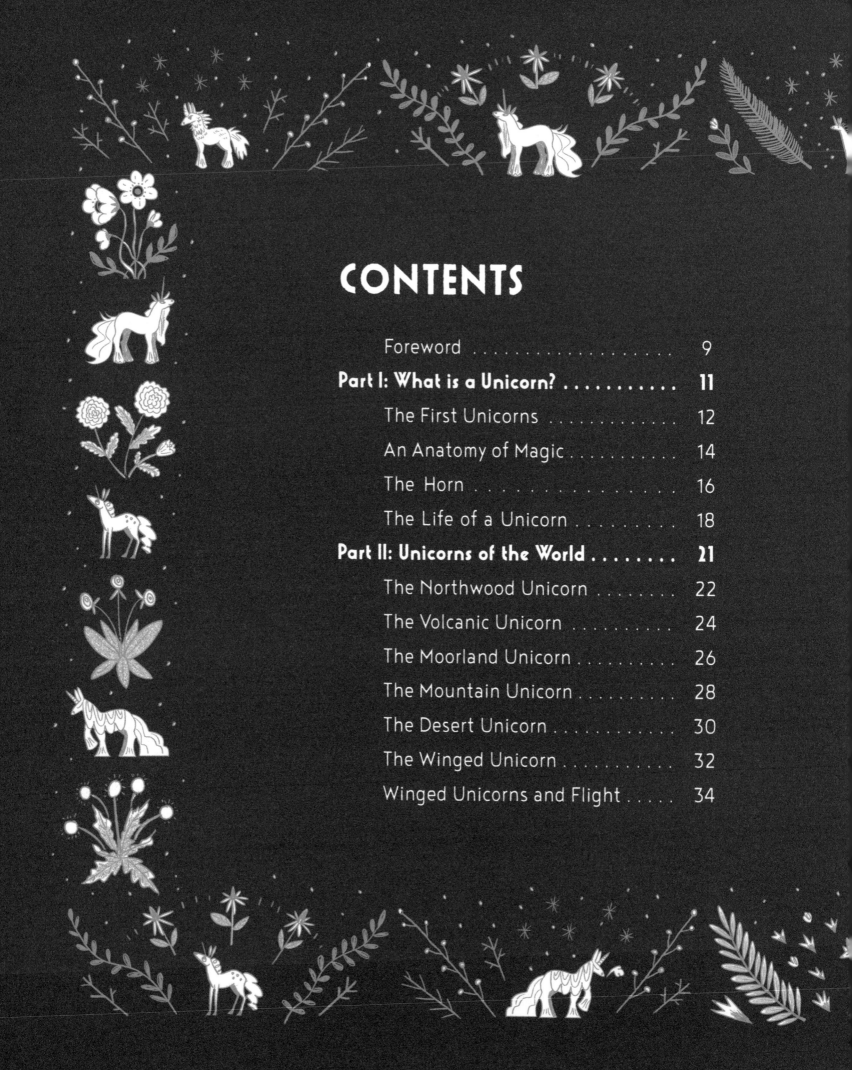

CONTENTS

Dear Reader,

My name is Dr Temisa Seraphini and I am the leading expert on unicornology.

Since life on Earth began, the unicorn has existed. It is a creature that is peaceful, wild and pure. I first saw a unicorn when I was six years old, running through a forest in England. I had taken a tumble and scratched my elbows and knees when a young unicorn with its horn barely grown appeared before me. It licked my swollen knee, then nudged me upwards and onto the path home before galloping away. From then on I spent every spare moment trying to learn more about these creatures.

My studies have taken me across the world and deep into the archives of the oldest libraries. I've researched every detail, sifted through the myths and separated the tall tales from the truth. In this book, you will discover the unicorn's importance in the world's myths and ancient arts, uncover the power of its magic, understand its evolution and learn how to protect it.

I hope these pages will guide you to understand the noble unicorn just as I have . . . and help bring it back to our world.

Yours,
Dr Temisa Seraphini

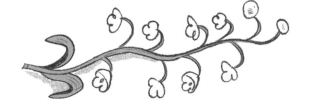

Part I
WHAT IS A UNICORN?

The unicorn is a hoofed herbivore of the Unicornuus family. A herbivore is an animal whose diet consists of only plants. Unlike its cousin the horse, unicorns also hold magical properties.

Unicornologists like myself study and track unicorns to better understand their ancestry, nature and magical properties. But the first unicorns did not resemble the ones we know today. Let's delve deep into the past and go back to a time when the Earth had not yet been trodden on by the earliest humans, to the first traces of the unicorn . . .

Taxonomy Chart:
Kingdom: Animalia | Phylum: Chordata | Class: Mammalia
Order: Artiodactyla | Family: *Unicornuus*

The First Unicorns

There are six different species of unicorn, and although they all belong to the same family, they can look very different from one another. The features that make them distinct have evolved over time to help them adapt to different environments.

Perisodactylla
Eocene: 54.8 – 33.7 mya[+] | Height: 0.6 m
An ancestor of the modern horse, rhinoceros, tapir and unicorn.

[+] Million years ago

Fabulaeractyls
Oligocene: 33.7 – 23.7 mya | Height: 0.8 m
Larger than *Perisodactylla*, *Fabulaeractyls* had still not developed a horn.

Baluchitherium
Miocene: 23.7 – 5.3 mya | Height: 1.2 m
A small horn had started to develop on the *Baluchitherium*.

2 m

1.8 m

1.4 m

1.2 m

0.8 m

0.6 m

0 m

Height
in metres

Cornumagnatopalys

Pliocene: 5.3 – 1.8 mya | Height: 1.4 m

After enduring an ice age, close ancestors of *Unicornuus*
developed a thicker hide and mane to endure the cold.

Unicornuus

Pleistocene: 1.8 mya – present day | Height: 1.8 m

Much taller than its ancestors, the modern unicorn has
a fully formed muzzle and jaw, and a distinct horn.

An Anatomy of Magic

There are several parts of a unicorn's body which possess magical properties. Each part has a particular power and, when used in the right way, can be extremely potent.

Horn

A unicorn's horn is known for its ability to neutralise poisons and grant long life. Great kings and queens often had goblets made of horn, and when visiting foreign lands or great banquets, they would only drink from unicorn horn goblets.

Tail

A unicorn's tail grows between 60 cm and 120 cm long. The hair is so wiry and strong that three strands plaited together are as sturdy as iron, making it ideal for armour. Only a blade forged in the fire of a volcano can pierce it. Its strength is at its greatest when the hair has been presented by the unicorn itself.

Eyes

Unicorn tears can be used to heal the sick. Given freely, they can heal the gravest wound, but if taken by force their properties weaken and they become ineffective against even a light fever.

Nose

Unicorns are highly sensitive to smell and use this sense to paint a mental picture of everything within a 50 km radius. They can smell fear, anger and good or ill intentions, but most importantly the purity of one's heart. They are able to detect humans before they come too close.

Blood

A life source that could give unimaginable strength to those that drank it, the most cruel and devilish of hunters would slay the unicorn to drain it of its blood.

The Horn

Perhaps the most iconic feature of a unicorn, the horn emerges from the front of its head, and comes in three distinct varieties.

Types of Horn

Made from bone, the horn grows from the skull in a similar way to deer antlers. The bone grows weaker with age and eventually the horn drops off soon before a unicorn dies. There are three types of horn; ridged, smooth and pearlescent. Ridged horns twist as they grow, forming a shape not too dissimilar to a turret seashell. Smooth horns taper down to a very sharp, fine point and tend to be thinner than ridged horns. Pearlescent horns can be ridged or smooth, but have a soft blue sheen. They have only been identified on the Winged unicorn species.

Ridged / Mountain   **Pearlescent / Winged**   **Ridged / Volcanic**

Smooth / Moorland   **Smooth / Desert**   **Smooth / Northwood**

Discovery

It wasn't until 1858 that Dr Ninny Colette discovered that a unicorn's horn falls off its head before death. While closely examining what she believed to be the skull of a horse, Dr Collete discovered the tiniest of ridges forming a rough circle on the forehead. Closer inspection revealed that the inside of these ridges contained fibres that were not bone. Something had sat within this delicate cavity - Dr Collete realised she was holding none other than a unicorn skull! Her suspicions were later confirmed when she discovered the exact missing horn.

Maintenance

The unicorn has developed a clever method to both clean and sharpen its horn at the same time. Using the bark of a tree, it gently grates the edge of its horn against the trunk. The friction gives its horn a knife-like sharpness whilst also grinding away dirt and residue.

The Life of a Unicorn

Although there is still much to be discovered about the life cycle of unicorns, recent observations have allowed us a much deeper understanding of their development and growth.

Pregnancy and Birth

The gestation period, or the time that the fetus is inside its mother, varies between 8 and 11 months depending on the species. A young unicorn looks much like the foal of a horse as it does not produce a horn until it is at least three months old. At this stage a small stump begins to appear, which can take up to another three months to fully form into a horn.

Youth

Within a year, the young unicorn is almost at full size and weight. During this time, it stays close to its family and travels in a herd (known as a blessing). Both the mother and father show it how to forage, how to camouflage itself and most importantly, how to avoid animals, including humans, that might cause them harm.

Mating

As it reaches maturity, the adult unicorn searches for a partner. Once it finds a match, it bonds for life.
In the unicorn family, the male and female do not seem to have any fixed role and each family is different.
Both have roles as protectors, nurturers, gatherers, fighters and teachers for their young.

Aging

Unicorns typically live between 60 and 80 years. A few months before
death, their horns fall off and for a season or two they are able to roam
free from human curiosity, without fear of capture. Although many
humans will often mistake them for a horse, unicornologists know
how to spot a unicorn by its size, markings and cloven hoof.

Part II

UNICORNS OF THE WORLD

The six species live in vastly differing habitats across the world. They can be found on the craggy slopes of Mount Everest or the hot, dry sands of the Sahara. These habitats have created some peculiar features which mark one out from the other.

We unicornologists have asked many questions about why those locations are important. What is it about the volcanic territory of Iceland, or the Northwood forest of the Americas? One thing that is certain is that these spots are ones of extreme beauty, filled with natural wonders and an abundance of life.

The Northwood Unicorn

The Northwood unicorn lives in the wild wooded terrains of North America and has become well-adapted to the changeable climate. Its hooves become sponge-like in the summer months and harden during winter. Its hair is hollow, which helps with flotation when swimming across the many rivers that divide the forests. It is the only species to migrate southward in winter.

Location: Canada and Northern territories of America
Hair: Short, coarse
Colouring: Brown, white, chestnut or black

Horn:
Smooth

Diet:

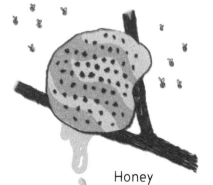

Honey

Wild flowers

Grass

The Unicorn of Ice

There was a time when Lake Itasca in Minnesota brimmed so full with water that the surrounding land became an expanse of bog and marsh. Further south along the continent the ground remained hardened and dry. According to legend, the Northwood unicorns gathered together and used their horns as ice picks to carve out a path where a river could flow. They worked for weeks cutting through rock, snow and clay to release the waters of the swollen lake and allow it to reach new areas. The result is a great river which now drains out across 33 states in North America.

The Volcanic Unicorn

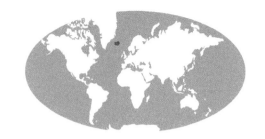

The Volcanic unicorn makes its home in the scenic landscapes of the Golden Circle in Iceland. This is a place that breathes magic, where wild plains sprawl between volcanic mountains and water rises in yellow-green mists. The Volcanic unicorn is typically stocky, short-legged and well adapted to the cold. It has a rugged coat and fringes of hair around the chest and hooves. It creates a mucus-like sweat which tangles into the hair and creates a barrier against icy winds.

Location: Iceland
Hair: Long, thick
Colouring: Pure white

Horn:
Ridged

Diet:

Grasses

Pine needle resin

The Protecting Unicorn

Legend has it that when the time comes for the volcanoes to unleash their fiery ash into the skies, four appointed Volcanic unicorns will gallop across the world and warn of the dangers to come. The Huldufólk of Iceland, (elf-like creatures who live in burrows of rock), first foretold this tale, and have collected untold volumes of information on this species. Their complex network of libraries is fiercely guarded and it was only with much perseverance that I was able to glimpse a few pages and take some precious notes on the diet and behaviour of the Volcanic unicorn.

The Moorland Unicorn

The Moorland unicorn is sleek and strong with a muscular body and a large set jaw. Its weight means it moves slower than some of the other species. When racing across the moors, it pushes its hind legs deep into the ground. The resulting sound of the Moorland in full gallop is like a deep drum roll.

Location: Northern Europe
Hair: Short with long flowing mane, tail and lower legs
Colouring: White, grey, chestnut and pure black

Horn:
Smooth

Diet:

Wild nettle

Grass

Mint

Heather

Bilberries

The Giving Unicorn

Unicorn hair was once woven into clothes for great kings and queens. According to mythology, when the small rocky island of Scotia came under attack from a neighbouring kingdom, Queen Trudy led an army to the cliffs of Grugghem. Around her, she wrapped a cloak of rare jewels and flaming gold, and spun within the lining was the precious hair of a Moorland unicorn. When the enemy armies came forth to shower down their fiery arrows, the robe of unicorn hair cast a vast shield around the queen and her people. In a moment of quiet, the sun appeared above the stormy rims and its rays shone against the sheen of the glossy cloak. It created a light so piercing that it seared the air and blinded the enemy. The fighters of Scotia leaped forward, throwing sharply-cut boulders out to sea so that the enemy's ships were shattered. The surviving ships took to the wind and retreated away from the island, defeated.

The Mountain Unicorn

Despite being one of the smallest varieties, the Mountain unicorn has incredible strength. Enduring some of the harshest conditions, it has developed a long, thick mane which hangs down its left flank. In the dead of winter, when the winds cut bitterly through the air, groups of Mountain unicorn huddle together, shoulder to shoulder. The mane warms the exposed flank of the unicorn next to it, and they shift their formation often so that no single unicorn is left to endure the cold for long.

Location: Tibet, Nepal and north-western China.
Hair: Long, thick
Colouring: White, sometimes streaked with dusty red or grey

Horn:
Ridged

Diet:

Shrubs

Berries

Grass

Dried leaves and plants

The Healing Unicorn

The hill folk of the Gansu region use powder of the Mountain unicorn's horn to create a spicy soup alongside aromatic herbs and hair. It is thought the healing properties can slow down signs of ageing and restore health. The great hermit Cantos, who has dwelled in the caves of Gansu for over 600 years, is said to drink this soup once a day.

The Desert Unicorn

The Desert unicorn lives on the dry, sandy dunes of Africa. It has adapted to the sweltering heat of the landscape by growing a very thin, glossy coat and a long, thin tail. Similar to camels, it also has thick eyelashes to keep out the sand, and its hooves are slightly flatter and wider to help it walk across the sand. It is the fastest and most ferocious of the unicorn species.

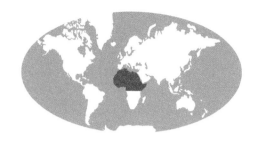

Location: Northern Africa and Egypt
Hair: Short with a bristly mane
Colouring: Varying from a light brown to a rich red

Horn:
Smooth

Diet:

Cactus bark

Shrubs

Doum palm nut

The Unicorn of Fire

Legend has it that when the Great Drought came over the land around 4,200 years ago, all living things suffered from the intense heat of the sun. Months passed with no clouds or rain. Flowers withered and blew away like ash. Animals grew sick and lay down on broken and tired legs. A young Desert unicorn, looked out at the land and his heart grew heavy from the misery he saw. There was little he could do, but he galloped to each dying flower and each crumbling animal, and asked them

gently, 'tell me your story'. As he listened, tale after tale followed him, and the wind at his heels picked up speed. The Desert unicorn ran so fast his hooves set alight, and the fires chased him with greed. He galloped so far and heard so many stories his heart grew heavy and shattered. As it broke, it extinguished the fire that had followed him, sending it searing up to the clouds which battled back down with rain. That is the story of how the Great Drought ended and why the Desert unicorn's hair is coloured a fiery red.

The Winged Unicorn

The most spectacular and the rarest species to spot is the famous Winged unicorn. Also known as an alicorn, it is the smallest of the six species. It is incredibly hard to gather information about them as they have never been sighted in the same place more than once. We still don't know how they breathe at such high altitudes, navigate their flight paths or stay warm while in the air. However, new and advanced technology is helping us to push forward in the mission to discover more.

Location: Unknown
Hair: Short, glossy
Colouring: Pure white or pale blue

Average wing span:
Approximately 3.7 m

Horn:
Pearlescent

Average feather length:
Approximately 18 cm

The Flight of the Winged Unicorn

Madame Caroline is the only person to have recorded the flight of the unicorn. Though she was not formally trained as a unicornologist, she was a great mechanic, and in 1923 created a set of aerodynamic wings in order to search for the Winged unicorn. Madame Caroline spent weeks high above the clouds studying the species. She disappeared soon after her longest flight. Recent papers have revealed that she was on the brink of a groundbreaking discovery.

Winged Unicorns and Flight

Madame Caroline was able to record the flight of Winged unicorns using a specially constructed speed gauge. She attached this to herself whilst following the unicorns in flight. The fastest recorded flying speed was 120 kmph, though she was certain that they could go much faster if needed.

Taking Flight

To take flight, the unicorn begins to gallop, building up extraordinary speed. Its powerful legs allow for great acceleration, and once enough speed is gained it must propel itself off the edge of a cliff or mountain edge. The unicorn momentarily dips beneath the ridge as though it has fallen, before its great wings catch the wind and carry it upwards. It is then able to beat the air as it rises in a graceful arc towards the sky.

Descent

This is the trickiest part. The unicorn must slowly make its way downward in a circular motion, reducing speed before hitting the ground. Its legs, which are usually tucked tightly beneath its belly during flight, unfold a few metres above ground. If they land whilst at speed, they can seriously damage their legs. If they reduce their speed too much, they risk losing the tread of air which keeps them gliding forwards.

Unicorn Atlas

The first map of unicorns created in 1609 by Dr Daichi, marked out the known locations of unicorns across the world. This was the beginning of a comprehensive study of their environment and the geographical significance of their locations.

Part III
UNICORNS and HUMANS

When I first began studying unicorns, I thought that my search to find out more would be difficult. I soon found that unicorns were not as mysterious as I imagined. They galloped across plains, drank from village wells and grazed side by side with other animals. In the murky passages of history, there are encounters that stretch back to our earliest civilisations. Humans revered and worshipped the unicorn, we welcomed them into our history and painted them into our stories. But the truth is that our relationship has not always been a pleasant one. Our thirst to tame the untameable drove the unicorn away, and magic fizzled out of existence . . . or so we thought.

In 1855, a professor called Ewan Stuart discovered a land which was filled with creatures he had thought long gone. He called it the 'Realm Beyond'.

Unicorns of Legend

The stories we tell and the way we tell them have always been a fascinating way to understand the past. Unicorns have poked their way through the myths and legends of history. They have appeared to different people and in different ways across every part of the globe.

The Messenger

1270 CE: Sleipnir was the great messenger of Odin, the Norse god of wisdom and war. It is said that Sleipnir was born when the realms of Valhalla and Midgard were still being built. With the strength of his twelve legs he could carry his rider wherever they desired – including the depths of the underworld.

The Fortunate

900 BCE: Known as the First Qilin in Ancient China,
this unicorn sought out a pact with a tortoise, a phoenix and
a dragon. Through this pact they agreed to bring good fortune
to any ruler that was worthy and make the land peaceful.

The Everlasting

200 CE: A wily and adventurous Winged unicorn once
flew too high trying to touch the light of the morning star.
He became trapped in the net of the sky and is for ever
framed as a constellation of stars known as Monoceros.

The Giver

1431 CE: This Moorland unicorn is named the Giver for the gift of hair she gave to Queen Trudy. Knowing that a fierce battle would take place, the Giver came to Queen Trudy and allowed her to pluck three hairs from her tail which would protect her.

The Unicorn in History and Art

Throughout history, there have been references to unicorns across art, architecture, scripture and folk tales. Here are some of the most famous references that I have come across in my research.

Mohenjo-daro

One of the oldest recordings of unicorns dates from 1700 BCE in the old city of Mohenjo-daro of the Indus Valley. Mohenjo-daro was one of the earliest and greatest civilisations in human history, stretching across what we now know as Pakistan and northern India, down from the Himalayas to the Arabian Sea. In the ruins of this great city, Dr Daichi uncovered clay tablets etched with the image of a unicorn.

Roman Empire

In 23 CE, the Roman historian Pliny the Elder took accounts from all sailors braving the uncharted seas. Among them were botanists and biologists who were travelling to discover foreign wilds. These adventurers reported all manner of beasts, including unicorns. Pliny wrote of them in his great work *Naturalis Historia*, the first natural history record to be compiled.

Ishtar Gate

In 575 BCE, in the region that is now Iraq, there once stood the great city of Babylon. The eighth gate that led into the city was richly decorated with lapis lazuli (a deep blue stone) and gold leaf. The wall bears the image of a lion, dragon and unicorn fiercely guarding the inhabitants of Babylon.

Taming of the Unicorn

Taming unicorns began in the Middle Ages, when world trade grew tremendously. During this time, there was demand for valuable goods, and materials were mined no matter what the cost. Unfortunately, the unicorn's precious magic was one of the most sought after items, so it was these gentle creatures who suffered most.

Cavalry

Some unicorns were captured and kept in orchards. Their keepers tried to train them into galloping or trotting at their command. They were intended to be used as cavalry and were tirelessly and ruthlessly worked by soldiers.

Ploughing

Some unicorns were hitched to wagons and made to plough fields. They toiled all day in intense heat, rain and snow. The farmers mistakenly believed their magic would produce delicious and bountiful crops.

Circuses

Others were made to perform in circuses for entertainment. Unicorns fought against lions in dusty rings, to the cheers of maddening crowds. Many were forced to take part in colourful parades, their captors showing off their prizes as they marched.

Medicine

Doctors would carry medical chests filled with ointments, balms and tinctures to a sick person's house, believing these remedies could cure illnesses. Among these items were nearly always samples of unicorn hair, horn powder and unicorn tears.

Famous Unicornologists

The greatest unicornologists have been immortalised and framed. Each professor was a pioneer in the research that has led to some our most fascinating discoveries.

Dr Haroh of Fire 1603 – 1662

Dr Haroh was one of the most gifted unicornologists in history. But despite her reputation as a protector of unicorns, she was a fierce lady who raged most of the day. Clouds of smoke followed her as she bristled and fumed. Her skin glowed an orange-red and her brow wrinkled in a mean crease. She was one of the last saviours of endangered unicorns, hiding them under her cloak of smoke, and is remembered for her fierce devotion to keeping the species alive.

Dr Daichi 1558 – 1615

Daichi was an avid sailor who crossed many oceans. He spoke 15 languages, which he used to communicate with people from all over the world, collecting their tales of unicorns. His gentle eyes soaked up all he discovered. He was known as the Great Messenger for the stories he recounted, and was the founder of the first Secret Society of Unicorns.

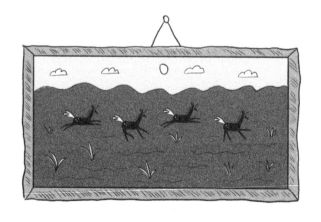

Dr Ewan Stuart 1772 – 1872

A man famous for speaking in riddles, to Dr Stuart, everything appeared backwards. A left turn took him the right way round, and a right turn took him straight ahead. It was through this ludicrous sense of the world that he managed to find himself accessing the magical Realm Beyond. He never knew how he slipped into it or wandered back out, but in that place he was able to record some of our most precious knowledge about magic and unicorns.

Dr Ninny Colette 1825 – 1897

This tall and robust archaeologist was never sick or affected by extreme weather, be it blistering heat or seething cold. Meticulous in her work, Dr Ninny Colette was rosy-cheeked, with a cheery disposition. She was the first to discover that the unicorn's horn falls off before its death. From that point on, Ninny dedicated herself to advancing research in the evolutionary history of unicorns.

Madame Caroline 1912 – 1961

Madame Caroline did not study in the traditional way, but learned by seeing, understanding and most of all believing. Her dedication to knowing more about the Winged unicorn brought her closer to the species than any other unicornologist.

The Realm Beyond

It was 1849 and an unseasonably warm summer. Dr Stuart was busy taking dung samples in the meadows of the higher alps when he noticed deep hoof impressions scattered wildly across the ground. These impressions were undoubtedly unicorn, but he simply couldn't tell where they had come from. For two years, Dr Stuart monitored the area but to no avail. During this time, he hypothesised that there must be a space which unicorns could enter and exist that was invisible to the human eye.

It wasn't until 1855 that he noticed a steady decline in the number of spruce trees growing in his observation area. He set about replanting these and just as he was finishing up for the day, he saw a shimmer in the air and a glint of light coming from between the trees. When he stepped towards it he found to his astonishment that a place appeared, filled with creatures he had thought long gone.

'It was extraordinary. There was nothing visibly different from this place and our own world. The trees were still a yellow-green and the sky was blue, but a warm electric current seemed to sit heavily in the air. It was magic. A place of magic filled with those things that needed it most.'

Dr. E. Stuart, 1855

Another Hope

When hunters targeted unicorns during the Middle Ages, a new league of fighters formed to protect them. These fighters created the first Secret Society of Unicorns, known as the SSU. Their mission was a simple one – to track, observe and protect unicorns. Each secret society was led by a prominent unicornologist who distributed their messages through heavily encrypted channels.

United Kingdom Coat of Arms

Societies Around the World

The most famous SSU is found on the island of the United Kingdom. Even today you can find evidence of its existence in the country's coat of arms, which depicts the lion and unicorn together. This SSU was one of the first great houses to take up the call and soon many others followed. You can find unicorns on the arms of Ramosch in Switzerland, Saint-Lô in France, Líšnice in the Czech Republic, Schwäbisch Gmünd in Germany and Nova Scotia, Canada. In Scotland, the society was so powerful it became a symbol of their land - it is their national animal!

These societies are the last standing guard, monitoring movements and sending messages through secret channels to different alliances across the world.

Saint-Lô Coat of Arms

Schwäbisch Gmünd Coat of Arms

How to Track a Unicorn

Wild unicorns still exist today, but their numbers are so few and they are scattered so far across the world that sightings are rare. Tracking a unicorn is an exercise in stealth and patience. You must sit still and listen, taking note of all that is around, from what the trees are whispering to where the birds are flying.

1.

2.

3.

4.

5.

6.

7.

Kit List

1. A lightweight waterproof backpack   **2.** A cloak to keep you warm   **3.** A waterproof layer or an umbrella
4. A vial for collecting and storing unicorn hair   **5.** Some bread to feed the birds (you can listen to their calls for clues)
6. A notepad, pen and pencil for recording details   **7.** Dried fruits for you and the unicorn - if you chance upon it!

Look for signs...

Next time you venture into the forest, take a look at your surroundings. There are clues everywhere.

Trees: If you find marks across the trunk similar to these, you can be sure that a unicorn was once there, sharpening its horn in the very same spot as you.

Footprints: The unicorn's hoof looks similar to a goat's, but is larger in size. Look at the ground and see what sort of impressions have been left in the mud or grass.

Vegetation: Are there plants around that a unicorn may eat? Unicorns do not often stop in a single spot for long, except when feeding.

Understanding Unicorns

Just as humans do, unicorns use a range of expressions, movements and sounds to express their feelings. Short, gruff snorts show they are uncomfortable, whilst a drawn out whinny can be a sign of excitement or delight. Remember everything you have learned about unicorns – this knowledge is important in being able to approach them.

1.

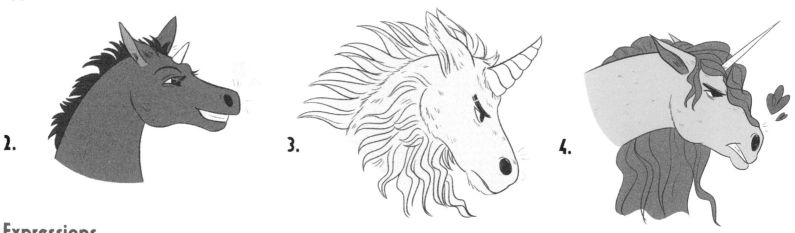

2.   **3.**   **4.**

Expressions

1. Ears pricked up – sensing danger, anxious   **2.** Ears twitching – excitable   **3.** Ears laid back – shy, feeling uncertain or intimidated   **4.** Bearing teeth – angry (do not approach if a unicorn bears its teeth)

1.

2.   **3.**

Body Language

1. Leaning forward and licking the hand – acceptance, trust has been gained

2. Swishing the tail – can indicate boredom   **3.** Stamping the legs – shows frustration

56

Communicating with Unicorns

The call of the unicorn is a wonder to encounter. If you really want to bring yourself close, you have to learn how to communicate. Unicorns are able to communicate with humans through telepathy, but it takes a trained human mind to do this effectively.

Step 1: Begin peacefully and calmly. Remove all thought from your mind. You must enter into a space of nothingness.

Step 2: Slowly step towards to the unicorn. It is important that you have achieved the first step in order to come close.

Step 3: Calmly and quietly introduce yourself to the unicorn. Project your thoughts toward it.

Step 4: Keep your thoughts centred on the deed at hand. If you simply wish to draw its markings and make note of its behaviour, then do this without losing focus.

A New Wild World

The unicorns' greatest danger now is that their world is no longer what it used to be. Their habitats, like those of many other animals, are being destroyed.

Can't they move?

Unicorns have evolved over thousands of years to be just right for their environment. Through our observations, we know what unicorns like to eat and where they like to live. We must look at forests, moors, deserts and mountains, see what once grew there, and replant it. But be aware that this will take time. It takes hundreds of years for a tree to stretch upwards, and only a few short minutes to cut it down.

Can't they eat something else?

Unfortunately not. You wouldn't expect a fish to bite through an apple or tiger to dine on plankton. Each species has developed a unique diet that is just right for their body. What we must do is create a new wild world, one which unicorns would be happy to return to.

What else can I do to help?

If on your quest to find unicorns you come across bits of plastic or rubbish, you can be sure that unicorns aren't likely to be around. You can help by removing rubbish and taking care of the environment.

Continuing the Journey

The unicorn has appeared everywhere in our history. In libraries throughout the world you will find them cleverly integrated into books and cunningly woven into pictures. The fear has always been that this information can be used for harm, but the time has now come when we must trust in good. Me and my team of committed researchers have begun the journey, but there's still work to be done. Armed with this knowledge, it's up to you to make a change. Take up your backpacks, sharpen your pencils, tell those you meet. *The Secret Lives of Unicorns* is just the beginning. Join me and maybe one day they will return to our side . . . and a little more magic will seep back into our world.

I would like to thank my fellow professors for all the support and encouragement they gave me in my research. It was not always easy to track down the precious nuggets of information that have found their way into this book. I would also like to thank the faraway believers for their quiet faith and the magical minds at Flying Eye who wanted the truth to be published. In particular I would like to thank my dear friend and teacher Dr Harold Birkinshaw for his unwavering belief and the sparkling revelation that we must never lose magic once we find it.

Yours,
Dr Temisa Seraphini